neopets

The Grey Faerie Chronicles:
Nomi's Quest

Neopets: The Grey Faerie Chronicles: Nomi's Quest
NEOPETS, and all characters, logos, names and related indicia are trademarks of NeoPets, Inc.
All rights reserved. Used with permission © 2008 NeoPets, Inc. NeoPets is a MTV Networks company.

Library of Congress catalog card number: 2007942249
ISBN 978-0-06-143214-9

Book design by Joe Merkel
❖
First Edition

neopets

The Grey Faerie Chronicles:
Nomi's Quest

Written by **Vivian LaRue**
Illustrated by **The Neopets Art Team**

NICKELODEON

HARPERFESTIVAL®
A Division of HarperCollinsPublishers

Nomi sat on her favorite cloud, absentmindedly twisting a lock of fiery red hair around her finger. Her wings fluttered in the gentle breeze as the cloud bobbed up and down over Faerie City.

She was waiting for her mentor, Mayin. Nomi didn't get much time to think—between studying and helping Mayin with her tasks—so she was relishing these few moments of peace. From where Nomi sat, she could see the tops of Faerie City's majestic buildings peeking above some of the lower clouds. The golden peaks were twinkling in the sunbeams; colossal domes dominated the horizon with their grandeur.

No matter how many times she saw this view, Nomi never stopped being impressed by it. *There's just no place like Faerie City,* she thought. Looking up into the bright blue sky, Nomi was reminded of the day she had learned that Mayin was going to take her on as her apprentice. On a day as perfect as this one, Nomi had anxiously waited for a very special letter to be delivered.

Three months before that day, Nomi had sent a letter to Mayin, asking her to be her mentor. All faeries Nomi's age apprenticed to a mentor faerie. For as long as she could remember, Nomi had dreamed of learning from Mayin, who had a reputation for being patient and fair and deeply gifted as a mentor. Many powerful faeries had studied under her. Nomi was certain that, with the right training, she could be as great as they were one day!

Nomi had always been a hard worker, and she had no trouble learning spells. Practicing them at home, she found that they rolled off her tongue as easily as her own name. But no matter how hard she studied, when it came to performing the simplest acts of magic, she faded. Nomi just knew that Mayin could teach her how to be the powerful faerie she had always dreamed of becoming. And so she had poured her soul into the letter, hoping against hope that she would be chosen.

Once the letter was sent, there was nothing to do but wait. Day after day, Nomi would nestle into her favorite nook by the window with a book in hand, and study spells until the sun went down. As the weeks passed with no response, Nomi began to find it harder and harder to focus on her studies. She caught herself glancing up at every passerby, hoping to spot the mail faerie carrying the letter that would seal her fate.

Finally the day came.

As soon as she caught sight of the winged faerie with the blue satchel rounding her corner, Nomi flew outside to meet her.

"Anything for me?" she asked.

"Oh! Let's see," the mail faerie replied. "Nalor, Nessivia, Nimbletoes . . ."

"Nomi, the name is N-O-M-I," she said.

"Noma?" asked the mail faerie as she peered through her spectacles at a golden envelope. The mail faerie loved to tease Nomi. By now, she knew what Nomi was waiting for—she had been just as worried when she was Nomi's age. At last, she handed over the gilded packet to Nomi with a wink.

"Good luck, dear!" she said, and zoomed off to her next delivery.

Nomi stared at the envelope. Too scared to open it, she flew back into her house and tucked herself safely into her little corner. A thousand thoughts swirled around her head: *What if Mayin doesn't agree to be my mentor? What if despite all my hard work, she doesn't think I'm good enough?*

With trembling hands, Nomi tore open the envelope, unfolded the letter, and began to read.

Dear Nomi,

Thank you for your letter. As I'm sure you can imagine, I receive so many inquiries at this time of year. Please do accept my apologies for the delayed response.

There are many qualities I look for when selecting an apprentice: a superior knowledge of spells, a meticulous approach to studying, and a mastery of magic. The bond between apprentice and mentor is very strong. Each year I must choose wisely.

I must confess that your lack of magical skills gave me some cause for concern. But after reading your letter many times, I have decided to take a chance on you. Your unwavering passion far surpasses anything that can be learned. I believe you possess an exemplary dedication to becoming a great faerie.

Therefore, it is with pleasure that I invite you to become my apprentice! Kindly meet me at Gaelyn Hall at 8:00 sharp next Monday morning so that we may begin our studies together.

Very sincerely yours,

Mayin

An overwhelming sensation of relief surged over Nomi, and she noticed that her whole body was trembling. She flopped into her favorite lavender chair and reread the letter. Slowly, the reality of her future began to sink in. She was going to learn magic from one of the best mentors in Faerie City!

"Ready to go, Nomi?" Mayin called as she flew up to the cloud. Mayin was always on time and expected the same of her apprentices.

"Oh! I didn't see you coming," Nomi said with a start.

Mayin gave Nomi an appraising look, taking in the lock of hair wound tightly around her finger. "What's on your mind?" she asked. "You're thinking about the Faerie Festival again, aren't you?"

How does she always know what I'm thinking? Nomi tried to unfurrow her brow as she let go of the twisted lock of hair. "The Faerie Festival?" she repeated, waving her hand in front of her face. "I'm not worried about *that.*"

But of course she was. Nomi had been thinking about the festival every day and every night since Mayin had told her about the special ceremony.

"All the junior apprentices will be performing acts of magic," Mayin had explained. "They will be competing for the Faerie Queen's Peridot Crown, the prize for the best presentation."

Of course, once she knew about the competition, Nomi couldn't go anywhere without hearing other apprentices buzzing about it. Everyone knew the crown was the ticket to winning the respect of the entire faerie community. Nomi craved that respect more than anyone. And she was desperate to prove to Mayin that she was worthy of the faith she had placed in her.

"Have you started thinking about what you'll do for the competition?" Mayin gently asked as the cloud they were riding was caught by a gust of wind.

"No, I'm not sure what I'm going to do," Nomi said, stroking her petpet, Zizi, who had just poked her head out of her purse. The little Faellie looked up at her and purred. "All I know is that I have to win," she added under her breath.

Nomi had struggled all year to master simple and straightforward spells, so she was sure that no one would be expecting her to win any competitions. As much as she hated to admit it, she was jealous of some of the other apprentices who had an easier time learning magic.

"It's not always about winning," Mayin said reassuringly.

"I know," Nomi said. Then she shrugged. "Come on, let's fly. I still have a lot of raindrops to collect."

Mayin opened her mouth to say something, but then seemed to think better of it. "As you wish," she said mildly. "Florina asked me to pick up a book for her, so we'll need to make a quick stop at the Bookshop first."

Nomi nodded, then tucked Zizi back into her purse. "You always know just how I feel, don't you?" she whispered as she stroked the Faellie's large, soft ears. Zizi purred and snuggled into the purse as Nomi flew off beside Mayin.

Faerieland Bookshop was crowded today with a noisy hustle and bustle. A line snaked around the tables. Shoppers were eager to read the long-awaited sequel to the Battle Faerie's bestseller, *When All Else Fails*.

"Why don't you look around?" Mayin suggested. "I'll get in line for Florina's book."

Nomi was wandering through the shelves of books about Faerie folk, painting, spells, and magical technique when a familiar laugh rang in her ears. She ducked behind a shelf just in time to spy Tula and Jasin walking past with armloads of books.

Nomi had grown up with these faeries, although to look at them, no one would guess that they were all the same age. Tula was at least a head taller than Nomi. Even more aggravating to Nomi, though, was the fact that Tula never seemed to have to work at anything. Without ever cracking a book, she just picked up magic at lightning speed!

And Nomi could never figure out how Tula got her hair to stay perfectly in place no matter how fast she flew, or how she never wore the same dress twice, or where she got that sweet perfume that filled the air when she fluttered her wings. Things just seemed to come so easily to Tula.

Unfortunately, Tula's magical prowess was matched by her sharp tongue. All the apprentices did their best to cozy up to her, since one wrong move could lead to a lifetime of being the target of Tula's catty quips.

Tula's best friend, Jasin, was always right by her side. She, too, towered over Nomi, and she shared Tula's gift for spells. Actually, Nomi suspected that Jasin's power was even greater than Tula's, although Jasin would never have allowed Tula to discover that. Nomi guessed that she, like most, was terrified of getting on Tula's bad side.

When they had first met, all those years ago, Nomi had tried to be friendly, but Tula and Jasin had made it very clear that she was not in their league. So now she did what any sensible faerie would do and avoided them as much as possible.

This wasn't always easy, since Tula and Jasin were studying under Tamerin, a powerful faerie who happened to be a close confidante of Mayin's. These days, it was almost impossible for Nomi to avoid the close-to-perfect-and-not-so-friendly Jasin and Tula.

Recently, Mayin had assigned her the task of trapping raindrops for Florina, the powerful faerie who oversaw Faerieland's mentoring program. Nomi had arrived at the

North Cloud only to discover that Tula and Jasin were already there, busily gossiping as they coaxed raindrops into their canisters. She had sought out a remote corner to work in, and tried to concentrate on filling her canister. *The sooner it's full, the sooner I can get away from them,* she had told herself. But she couldn't help overhearing Tula and Jasin when they began talking about the competition. The more Nomi tried to ignore them, the more she wondered about their conversation.

"If we can learn how to do a Sun Ray burst, our ending will be perfect, don't you think?" Tula had asked. "I doubt anyone else is doing that level of magic."

Jasin had nodded in agreement, as she always did.

Nomi had kept her head down and continued working. But all she could think about was winning that crown, and proving to these two faeries and the rest of Faerie City what she knew in her heart she was capable of.

Not that it would be easy. Compared to Tula and Jasin, Nomi knew her own magic looked pretty pathetic. So far, the most impressive spell she had accomplished was summoning a small lightning flash. She'd been excited about it until she'd spotted a much younger apprentice effortlessly pulling off the very same spell a day or two later.

Mayin rounded the corner with the new book and joined Nomi just as the two other apprentices left the shop. "I guess they're working on their act for the competition," she mused as she watched the giggling faeries fly away.

Nomi just rolled her eyes.

"Did you find anything interesting?" Mayin asked. Nomi shook her head and they walked through the rows of books together. Suddenly Mayin stopped and pointed to a book propped on a lower shelf: *The Faerie's Guide to Simple Spells.*

"Let's get that for you! Maybe you'll find something in it for the festival," she suggested.

"*Simple spells!*" Nomi snorted. "Maybe I need a book on luck instead."

Mayin gently patted Nomi's arm.

"Nomi," she said, "you have to relax about the competition. Before you head off for your task, why don't we treat ourselves to a faerie fondant?"

Instantly, Nomi was in a better mood.

Like most faeries, she wasn't one to pass up chocolate! Maybe a gooey, sticky treat was just what she needed to help her hatch a plan for the festival.

"Sure," Nomi said. "That sounds more exciting than trapping raindrops for Florina." Nomi hesitated for a second and then confessed, "I really don't see how that task is going to help me become more powerful, anyway!"

"Be patient," Mayin told her. "Florina always has her reasons. I know it's not easy to be a junior apprentice, but you need to trust me and all of the mentors. Everything you do for us will help you become more powerful in time." Mayin gave Nomi an encouraging smile. "If it helps any, I never was able to catch enough raindrops to fill that canister," she admitted.

Nomi smiled back. Somehow, Mayin always knew just the right thing to say.

"Let's go!" said Nomi as she took off.

Faerie City was crowded with faeries flying around, gossiping about the festival. The tall crystal buildings shimmered in the bright sun as Nomi and Mayin landed on a white cobblestone street. They made their way through the crowds, noticing all the colorful Faerieland flags announcing FAERIE FESTIVAL IN THREE WEEKS!

"I'm going to drop the book off at Florina's," Mayin said. "I'll meet you at Faerie Foods. Order me a fondant!"

Faerie Foods was a large tent at the far end of the open market in the eastern part of Faerie City. Here there were no tall buildings, just the billowing tents of the market vendors.

As Nomi flew to the market, Zizi burrowed her tiny head safely into Nomi's purse. There were many faeries flying and Zizi didn't like crowds.

At the food tent, a pretty faerie with green wings greeted Nomi.

"Hello," she said sweetly. "Welcome to Faerie Foods, where the food is from the heavens! How can I help you?"

Nomi scanned the glass case, her eyes dancing over the sorbets and freshly baked starry shortbread cookies. Just when she spotted the faerie fondants, she heard a familiar voice behind her. "Oh, Jasin, look who's here!"

Her heart sinking, Nomi turned around. *Can't I go anywhere without running into them?*

There stood Tula with her face pinched in a smirk. "It's the world's weakest faerie! Nomi, do you need some help carrying your food? It might be heavy!"

Jasin fluttered her wings and flashed Nomi a huge phony smile. "Hello, Flightning Bug."

"Hi," Nomi mumbled, wishing that she had the power to turn invisible. She whipped around to focus on her order, her cheeks burning red.

"I'd like two faerie fondants, please," she said to the faerie behind the table.

"What's the matter, Nomi?" Jasin taunted her. "Too busy to chat with your old friends?"

Zizi growled as she popped her head out of the purse and looked over at Jasin and Tula.

"Look," Jasin said, pointed to Zizi. "Even her petpet is puny!"

The two faeries shrieked with laughter as time slowed to a crawl for Nomi. She tried desperately to come up with a razor-sharp response, but as always, her mind went blank, and she just stood there blinking. Of course, later that night when no one was around to hear it, she was sure she'd think of the perfect comeback!

"Hi, Nomi," Mayin sang out as she flew into the tent. "Oh, good afternoon, Jasin. Hello, Tula," she greeted the others.

Everyone respected Mayin. Jasin and Tula would never dare say a bad thing about her. Mayin had such a natural way with magic, it stopped even these faeries in their flight.

"Hi, Mayin," Tula and Jasin sang sweetly in unison.

"I hope that you are both flying well," Mayin said politely.

"Yes, Florina asked us to deliver some

books to the Faerie Queen, so we're just on our way back." Jasin replied.

"Well, you'd better hurry back," replied Mayin. "It's never a good idea to keep Florina waiting."

"Two faerie fondants," the faerie behind the counter called out, handing Nomi the chocolate treats. "Careful, they're hot!"

Nomi took the treats and grabbed two spoons.

"Don't worry about them," Mayin told her, nodding in Jasin and Tula's direction as they left the tent.

Nomi dropped into a chair and dug into the fondant.

"It's just not fair," she mumbled through a mouthful of warm chocolate. "They have it so easy. I'd be happy if I had *half* their magic."

"If you study and practice, you can be a great faerie," said Mayin. "I've mentored many faeries before you, Nomi. And they have all become powerful and respected. You will, too, one day."

"One day isn't before Faerie Festival, is it?" Nomi asked hopefully.

"No, probably not," Mayin replied with her friendly wink.

Zizi licked a bit of chocolate off Nomi's hand and seemed to nod in agreement.

"Silly Zizi," Nomi cooed to her pet. "You love chocolate, huh?"

"Listen, Nomi, I've got to run," Mayin said. "The festival will be better than you think. You've worked so hard this year, and I know you're frustrated. But I promise, it's all going to come together for you!"

Nomi smiled a little sadly. "Thanks, Mayin," she said.

Mayin reached into her pocket and pulled out a small box. "I have something for you," she said. "I was going to give it to you after the festival, but I want you to have it now." She placed the box in Nomi's hand and then flew quickly out of the tent.

Nomi looked after Mayin, blinking in surprise. Then she turned her gaze to the small box. Carefully, she opened it. Inside, nestled on a cloud of soft cotton, was an intricately carved bracelet. On the outside, many-colored crystals sparkled. On the inside, a tiny inscription was carved: *For Nomi. Have the courage to believe in yourself! With love, Mayin*

CHAPTER TWO

The next day, Florina called Nomi into her private study in the early morning. Florina was flying around the room furiously. Whenever Florina was tense, she had the habit of flying in circles. It made Nomi a little dizzy.

"Please go see Reena, the faerie at the Rainbow Pool, and ask her for a vial of magic water. I'm all out and I need it for a spell that will change the color of the North Tower.

Someone has played a trick and made it invisible again." Florina said. "Tula and Jasin are going as well, so you'll fly together."

Nomi's heart sank. "I don't need Jasin and Tula to fly with me. I can go alone!" she offered.

But Florina barely heard her. "It's all arranged," she said. "I told Tamerin that you'd meet Jasin and Tula at the North Cloud in ten minutes."

Florina gave the young apprentice a distracted smile and flew quickly toward the door. "I have to rush off," she called as she departed. "I must get to Tamerin's for a festival planning meeting."

Nomi sighed and gathered the papers that Florina had blown on the floor with her fluttering wings. She was not looking forward to flying with Jasin and Tula. She would have rather gone on the journey by herself, but Florina hadn't really given her a choice. Nomi closed the door to Florina's study and started toward the North Cloud.

The Rainbow Pool was a beautiful place with a sparkling waterfall and sweet-smelling flowering trees. There was always a huge rainbow ending just over the cloud that reflected lively colors in the crystal-clear water. Normally, Nomi enjoyed any opportunity to speak with Reena, the beautiful and kind faerie who ran the pool and cared for the magic water. Reena was always generous to Nomi and made her feel special. But with Tula and Jasin along, even a trip to the Rainbow Pool felt like a chore.

As Nomi hovered over the North Cloud, she saw them approaching.

"Come on, Nomi," Tula called, barely slowing down her wings. "Hurry up. We're going to fly straight over the Cloud Bridge."

"What about over the Employment Agency? Isn't it faster?" Jasin asked.

Tula shot a sharp glance Jasin's way.

"Or perhaps we should just fly straight over the Cloud Bridge," Jasin corrected herself. No one liked to fight with Tula. She had a way of winning an argument.

Unexpectedly, Nomi found herself feeling a little sorry for Jasin. Sure, she had chosen to be Tula's shadow, but every faerie deserved a thought of her own. Nomi suddenly wished she had enough confidence to tell Jasin not to let anyone push her around. But today wasn't the day. They were on an assignment for Florina.

The three faeries continued on their way to the Rainbow Pool. The day was clear and bright; the perfect conditions for flying. Nomi loved to fly out in the open sky, feeling the breeze ripple her wings. If the wind was right, she could pick up a strong current and glide along peacefully for hours. For a moment, Nomi forgot all about the pressure of performing at the festival. Until Tula brought it up.

"Are you even going to be in the festival?" she asked as they all glided on the strong air current.

"I don't know yet," Nomi answered warily.

Just then a strong gust of wind took them by surprise, and Nomi struggled and flapped her wings frantically to stay on course. Tula and Jasin exchanged a smirk, but to Nomi's relief there was no more conversation.

At the Rainbow Pool there was a crowd of faeries and Neopets waiting for a chance to talk to Reena. A supervising faerie handed them a blue stone with a silver number and told them to wait until their number was called. Nomi sat down on the lush green lawn that surrounded the water and took out her sewing from her bag. She would never be as good at sewing as Mayin, but she could at least try to practice making her stitches even.

Jasin and Tula sat on a rock nearby. They didn't think that Nomi could hear them speaking, but Nomi heard every word.

"Have you heard about Edna the Witch?" Tula asked Jasin. "She lives in the Haunted Woods in a tower. I heard that she has special powers." Tula leaned in closer, lowering her voice. "Do you know Falin, that senior apprentice with the short, brown hair?"

Jasin nodded. "She's the one Tamerin called on last night to demonstrate the rules for travel and safety outside Faerie City, right?"

"Exactly," Tula said, smiling. "I hear that she has gotten more powers because she went to Edna. The old witch has powers to help light faeries increase their magic."

Nomi kept her eyes on her work, but her ears were keenly tuned to what Tula was saying.

Jasin's eyes widened. "Can she help us with the Sun Ray burst?

"That's the thing," Tula replied with a twinkle in her eye. "If we can get her to boost our powers, we can be the best act at the festival. With the Sun Ray burst as our finale, there's no way anyone could beat us." A smile spread across Tula's face. "Imagine what Tamerin would say if we won," she continued. "She'd make us senior apprentices right away.

No more running around doing these silly errands."

Jasin clapped her hands together. "And we'd get the Peridot Crown!" Then she stopped clapping. "But that means we'd have to go to the Haunted Woods." Jasin shuddered and wrapped her arms around her body. "I don't want to go there."

"Oh, come on, don't be such a baby," Tula scoffed. "It's not like we're powerless little faeries anymore. We could handle Edna." She stood up with her hands on her hips. "Don't tell me that you're afraid of the Haunted Woods?"

Jasin bit her lip. "Isn't the Haunted Woods where Balthazar lives?"

Every faerie had heard the rumors about Bathazar and how he hunted faeries for sport and coins. According to the stories, he patrolled the Haunted Woods, capturing faeries, shrinking them, and then trapping them in glass jars. He'd sell the little faeries to the highest bidder—no matter who they were.

"Whatever," said Tula with a dismissive toss of her head. "We don't need any old witch. We're so far ahead of all the junior apprentices. Just look at Nomi. She can barely fly straight! We have nothing to worry about."

Nomi's ears burned bright red when she heard this. She wished that she had advanced as quickly as Jasin and Tula. She was tired of being told to wait for her powers to develop. Maybe there was some truth to this rumor about Edna. She had seen Falin, and it was true that she was very advanced. Had she really made it all the way to the Haunted Woods to see Edna?

"You are totally right," Jasin said to Tula, relieved that there was no more talk about going to the Haunted Woods.

When they returned to the place on the lawn where Nomi was sitting, there was only one Kacheek ahead of them. As they waited for the Kacheek to finish, all Nomi could think about was how great it would be to arrive at the festival and surprise all of Faerieland with new abilities. What would everyone have to say about her then?

An idea began to take shape in Nomi's head.

When their turn came, Reena gave each apprentice a vial of the magic water and sent the young faeries on their way with a bright smile. Jasin and Tula stayed to visit with other apprentices on the lawn while Nomi ducked out of the scene and headed for the library to do some research. She'd heard spooky tales about the Haunted Woods and about Balthazar. But she didn't actually know where the woods were—or what to expect.

The library was in the middle of Faerie City. It was in an old stone building with beautiful stained glass windows. Inside, there were a few elder faeries reading in the front room. The faerie librarian looked up at Nomi as she flew in, and greeted her with a smile.

"Can I help you?" she asked.

"Yes," Nomi responded. "Where do you keep the reference books?"

If Nomi was pressed about what she was looking for, she figured that she could say she was on an errand for Florina.

"The third aisle, the last bookcase," the faerie responded.

Before the librarian could ask any questions, Nomi was off. She kept her head down and found her way to the reference bookcase. Fluttering her wings, she flew up to the top shelf. Tucked away on the high shelf was a large black leather-bound book with heavy gold letters embossed on the spine, *Maps of Neopia*. Nomi knew this book would hold the answers. She slid it off the shelf.

The weight of the book brought her crashing down to the ground. Several faeries and a few Neopets looked over. Nomi sat up quickly, rubbing her head. Then she waved, signaling that she was okay. The others went back to their reading while Nomi slid the book over to the table at the end of the aisle. With all her strength, she lifted the book onto the tabletop.

Making sure that no one was watching, Nomi turned the small table light on and opened the book. The pages were yellowed and frayed at the corners. The ancient book had a musty smell. Nomi guessed no one had opened it in the last century. She flipped through the pages until she found a map of the Haunted Woods. Nomi held her breath as she pored over the pictures on the map: the Deserted Fairground, Spooky Food, the Brain Tree. . . .

Finally, Nomi spotted Edna's Tower. Her heart quickened as she stared at the picture of Edna. She looked exactly as Nomi had imagined—green skin, dark cloak, and a small, pink nose. Nomi had never seen a Neopet like this in Faerieland. In fact, Nomi had never been outside the gates of her beloved city! *But what's the point of living in Faerieland if I can't even do faerie magic?*

Nomi thought. Gazing at the map, she toyed distractedly with the bracelet that Mayin had given her. And then, as clear as day, she knew what she needed to do.

It's time I had the courage to believe in myself.

She was going to the Haunted Woods, and she was going to meet Edna!

Nomi made sure that no one was watching her and then quickly tore the Haunted Woods map out of the book. She knew it was wrong, but there was no other way for her to find Edna's Tower. *Once Edna increases my magical power, I can put the map back, good as new!* she told herself. She carefully folded the map and tucked it into her purse. Then she hoisted the heavy book back to its spot as quietly as she could.

As she flew home, her heart beat quickly.

Edna could fill her with power so that she could perform at the festival—Nomi was sure of it!

Nomi dropped the magic water off at Florina's and then flew home quickly. Her petpet was waiting for her.

"Oh, Zizi," Nomi said, bending down to tickle her chin. "Everything is going to change!"

The little Faellie purred contentedly. Nomi was sad to leave her, but she knew that the journey would be much too dangerous for little Zizi.

The next morning, Nomi got up very early and packed up Zizi's food and favorite toys. "You're going to stay with Mayin for a day or two," Nomi whispered into Zizi's large ears as she stroked her soft fur.

Carrying her precious cargo, Nomi flew to Mayin's home, where she found Mayin's roommate, Domilla.

"Hi, Nomi," Domilla said, somewhat distracted. She was holding a faerie spell book in her hand. As she spoke, she didn't even look up from the page. "Sorry, Mayin isn't here. She has already left for her morning task."

Nomi was relieved. She felt badly enough not telling Mayin about her trip; lying to her face would have been twice as hard. She took a deep breath and blurted out the words she had rehearsed.

"That's okay," she said to Domilla. "Could you just tell her that I had to go on a trip for Florina and ask her to look after Zizi?"

Domilla looked up from the spell book. "Florina is sending you on a trip?" She peered at Nomi curiously and cocked her head to one side. "I never got to do that!"

Nomi shrugged and handed Zizi over with one last pat. Then she walked out and didn't look back.

Now nothing was going to stop her from seeing Edna and becoming a more powerful faerie.

CHAPTER THREE

Standing outside of Mayin's door, Nomi hesitated for a moment. But it was only a moment. Today Nomi's heart was full of the hope that she could gain more magical power.

The night before, Nomi had carefully planned her departure from Faerieland, plotting out a path where she was the least likely to be spotted. She couldn't risk running into anyone who might recognize her and question her—especially one of the other apprentices, or worse, a mentor. She had decided to take alleys and side streets and would leave before the early rush crowd.

The dew was still fresh and wet on the lawn of the Faerieland Employment Agency's waiting area as Nomi took flight. During the day, the lush lawn was bustling with Neopets socializing and mingling, but this morning it was peaceful and calm. Nomi flew low and skimmed the grass. The long green blades tickled her belly, and her heart felt light and airy.

Before Nomi knew it, she was at the edge of Faerieland. She decided that she should stop for a snack on the sandy beach before she began her journey over Neopia's wide, blue seas. Nomi sat down, opened her pack, and nibbled on the fire apple she had packed. She thought about what she would actually say to Edna when they met. Would she get tongue-tied? Scared? Her wings fluttered just thinking about it!

After a few minutes, Nomi strapped on her pack and took flight on a gust of wind moving over the sea. Nomi was silently thankful that it was a windy day. She would try to soar on the currents and save her energy for when she arrived at the Haunted Woods.

Sailing over the sparkling Neopian waters, Nomi wondered why more faeries didn't fly over the sea. It was beautiful! Buzzing over the water, she spotted a school of shimmering Koi and a sleek Flotsam. A little later, she even caught a rare sight of an Acara frolicking in the waves below.

Eventually, the sea gave way to solid ground. The land below the clouds looked dark and eerie. Nomi could see the crooked branches of trees and tall black iron gates reaching up toward the sky. The wind picked up and seemed to come at her from all directions, throwing Nomi off her rhythm of flight. She fought to stay on course. The long journey was beginning to make her weary.

As the old Deserted Fairground came into view, Nomi realized that she had arrived at the Haunted Woods. She wished that Zizi was there to keep her company. Inhaling deeply, she dived down closer to the ground.

A cold, gusty wind was blowing and the gates of the Fairground were clanging together. The place looked like it hadn't been open for business in years. Nomi had heard stories of the crazy Neopets who lived there. Peeking in, she saw only abandoned rides and decrepit, spooky games. It was the loneliest place imaginable. Nomi took hold of the gates and peered through the bars. Trying to get a better look, she squeezed her head through. Suddenly, Nomi was face-to-face with a pair of glaring red eyes!

As Nomi struggled to free herself from the bars, the shadowy creature began to sweep toward her. Desperately, Nomi twisted and turned, trying to get loose. Finally, she freed herself from the cold bars and fell backward, landing flat on her rump! Scrambling to her feet, Nomi flicked her wings and sped away from the Deserted Fairgound.

I guess it's not so deserted after all! Nomi thought as she flew.

Just then, Nomi heard a thunderous roar coming from the woods behind her. The ground shook as Nomi ducked behind a tree and covered her head. At first, she kept her eyes tightly shut. Then one eye opened. And then slowly she dared to open the other.

Nomi's heart jerked painfully in her chest. Right in front of her, an Eyrie perched among the branches, its hard, sharp beak just inches from her face! As Nomi froze, trying to decide whether to hide or flee, the Eyrie snapped its head toward her and twitched its long, furry tail.

"You," growled the Eyrie. "Who are you?"

Stunned, Nomi struggled to find her voice.

"I'm Nomi, from Faerieland," she whispered in reply.

"Why are you here?" asked the Eyrie in his slow-as-molasses drawl.

"I've traveled here to see a witch named

Edna. I need her help," was all Nomi dared to offer as a reply.

The Eyrie blinked its heavy eyes, obviously surprised. "Edna?" he repeated. "But she lives deep in the Haunted Woods!"

Nomi fluttered her wings nervously, not knowing what to say.

There was a long pause as the Eyrie glared at her. "Well, you're obviously not going to get there on your own," he finally said, sighing. "I'll help you reach Edna's Tower safely."

Nomi could hardly believe what she was hearing. "You'll . . . help me?" she stammered.

"Sure. I guess this is your lucky day," the Eyrie told Nomi. "My name is Krestyl, by the way."

The journey from the Deserted Fairground to Edna's Tower was a long one. It was nearly impossible for Nomi to fly among the twisted branches, so for the most part, they picked their way along the ground. Krestyl proved to be a patient guide, and Nomi often found herself wondering how she would have managed without him.

It was too difficult to talk as they walked along the narrow path, but their frequent rest breaks gave Nomi an opportunity to learn more about her surprising rescuer. "Why did you offer to help me?" she asked at one point, as they sat catching their breath on a gnarled stump.

"Well, I didn't have much choice, did I?" Krestyl joked. "It was either help you or let you die of fright at the first Lupe growl you heard."

Nomi giggled, then shook her head. "No, really," she persisted. "You didn't have to help me."

Krestyl shrugged. "Let's just say a light faerie did something nice for me once. It seemed like a good opportunity to return the favor."

Nomi sensed that Krestyl preferred to keep his past to himself, and she let the matter drop. "Come on," she said, rising and dusting off her dress. "Edna's Tower awaits!"

They continued on, and with every step Nomi grew more excited about her upcoming encounter with Edna, though she never did get used to being in the Haunted Woods. Even with a fearsome Neopet as her escort, she trembled when ghoulish calls echoed through the branches. And when she saw dozens of red eyes gleaming through the shadowy underbrush, she clung closely to Krestyl.

At last, they came upon a soaring stone tower.

"We've arrived!" Krestyl announced.

The two companions slowed their pace but

continued down the pathway to the tower, where Krestyl stopped. "We've safely reached the end of our journey," he said gently. "It's time for me to return home."

Nomi could barely remember why she had been so afraid of this kind beast. With a quiver in her heart, she flew up and nuzzled against the Eyrie's beak.

"Thank you, Krestyl. I will never forget your kindness," she said.

Krestyl gave her a gentle pat. "Be careful, Nomi," he said gravely. "Don't forget the witch can be tricky. And you never know who you can trust in these Woods."

Nomi began to walk toward the tower. Then she turned and waved. "Maybe our paths will cross again!" she said.

Krestyl held back a moment longer to watch Nomi make her way down the path to the tower. Then he turned and began his journey home.

At the bottom of the tower was an ancient wooden door with a heavy metal handle. To the left of the door was a raggedy broomstick. It looked like it had been there for centuries. Nomi looked around until she spotted a thick rope. She pulled on it a few times until a loud bell rang. A small wooden panel in the middle of the door slid open. Nomi couldn't see anyone's face, but she heard a deep, low voice.

"Who's there?" the voice called.

"My name is Nomi and I am here to see Edna," Nomi answered.

"Speak up!" the voice scolded. "I can't hear you."

Nomi flew up to the window.

"I am here to see Edna the Witch," she said

much louder. "I am Nomi, a light faerie from Faerieland."

"All right! All right! There's no need to shout," the voice boomed. "Hold on."

There was a loud bang and then the door slowly creaked open. It was dark inside the tower and Nomi hesitated for a moment.

"Well, are you coming in or not?" the voice asked.

Nomi flew inside and was surprised to see Edna herself standing in front of her. Her ears flopped out of her black hat, and her pink nose twitched as she examined her visitor. She looked just like the picture that Nomi had seen in the faerie library, only much shorter.

"You're Edna the Witch?" Nomi asked.

"The one and only," Edna said. She looked the young light faerie up and down. "What can I do for you?"

Nomi had thought about this moment the whole way to the tower, yet standing there she was suddenly too timid to speak. "I . . . I . . ."

"Oh, spit it out," Edna grumbled. "I don't have all day!"

"I have heard that you have special powers," Nomi blurted out.

Edna shot Nomi a shrewd glance and then began to cackle loudly.

"Yes, that is correct, indeed. I am quite powerful." She flashed Nomi an almost toothless grin and then continued, "Why exactly are you here? Why do you seek my power?"

Nomi took a breath, then confessed her deepest desire. "I would like to develop my magical powers more quickly. I heard you could help me," she said.

"I see. What is it with all you light faeries?" Edna mumbled. "Everyone wants to be stronger and better than the next! Must be something in the clouds these days."

Nomi's heart began to race. *It must be true!* she thought. *Others have come to see her!*

"Come," Edna ordered, motioning Nomi to follow her into the tower. She turned and walked to a spiral staircase at the rear.

Nomi carefully flew up behind Edna, squeezed herself into the staircase, and trailed her around the tiny metal winding steps, bumping her head every once in a while along the way. At the top, there was a door and Edna slowly turned the knob.

Nomi followed, her eyes struggling to adjust to the dark place. The only light came from a single tiny window, its ancient pane covered thickly with dust and cobwebs. A strong stench came from a large black bubbling cauldron in the corner. A long wooden table

stood at the back of the room with rows of jars full of different-colored specimens.

"Listen carefully. Here's how it works," Edna said, hoisting herself up on a stool. "I need some things from you before I can start the spell."

"What *things?*" Nomi asked tentatively.

"If you bring me back the ingredients that I ask for, I will help you." Edna said, grinning. "Simple, yes?"

"Yes," Nomi agreed. "Tell me what I need to do."

Edna nodded briskly. "I need a vial of black sand, two red poppies, and some purple juppie java."

"Purple juppie java?" asked Nomi.

"You heard me. Don't be foolish!" the witch snapped.

Nomi nodded, but she was confused.

She couldn't imagine how these things would help her become more powerful. Then she thought of beautiful Falin. Clearly, Edna's magic had worked on her! Nomi decided to trust Edna. After all, this was the whole reason she had made the journey to the Haunted Woods.

"All right," Nomi told her. "I'll get these things for you."

Edna picked up an empty vial. "You can find the black sand by the bank of the Demonica River and . . ." her voice trailed off. Nomi followed her gaze and saw a large Crokabek perched on Edna's tiny windowsill.

"Shoo! Shoo!" Edna shouted. "Get off my window! Every time I have visitors you show up and stare at me with your beady eyes. What a nuisance!" She walked toward the window, flapping her hands vigorously.

At Edna's approach, the Crokabek leaped from the windowsill and flew noisily away.

Edna thrust the empty vial into Nomi's hand. "Be quick about your task. I won't wait long for you." The witch cackled.

As the tower's wooden door slammed loudly behind her, Nomi thought about Edna's request. Black sand? Red poppies? Purple juppie java? How could these things help her gain power?

Nomi didn't know, but she was eager to find out. Determined to see her quest through, she set out once again into the unknown Haunted Woods.

CHAPTER FOUR

Nomi flew a short distance from Edna's Tower and then touched down in a small clearing. She needed a plan before she continued.

From her pack, she took out the map from the library book and smoothed the page out on her lap. She studied the Haunted Woods, looking for clues as to where to find the things that Edna had requested.

Right away Nomi spotted the tiny blue

squiggle that denoted the Demonica River. She was pleased to see that it was only a short flying distance from Edna's Tower.

She hoped the red poppies would be easy to spot in the woods. There certainly weren't many flowers growing in this dark place, so her chances seemed good.

For a moment, she thought that the witch might be playing a trick on her. But her thoughts went back to Falin's achievements. If Edna wanted black sand, red poppies, and purple juppie java, then that's what Edna would get!

Nomi glanced at the sky, trying to gauge what time it was. If she hurried, she could gather the ingredients for the witch's spell by sundown. Then she would have everything she needed, and Nomi could make her way back to Faerie City. Faerie City! Tears sprang to Nomi's eyes as she thought about Zizi and

Mayin. She hoped that they were not worried about her.

Taking to the air once more, Nomi felt a dull ache in her wings. The long journey had taken a toll on her, but she had no time to rest. She pressed on and soon spotted a sliver of black sand along the bank of a river. It was just as Edna had described it! She flew over to the edge of the water and took the empty vial from her pack. With great care, she filled the glass tube with black sand.

Nomi allowed herself a little smile. Maybe this wasn't going to be so hard after all! She tucked the vial of sand into her bag and prepared to set off in search of the red poppies.

Just as she was about to take flight, Nomi heard a whimper from behind a tree.

"Help!" a weakened voice called.

Nomi froze, her heart pounding.

"Is someone there?" the voice called again. "Can you help me?"

Nomi stood still as a statue, unsure of what to do. She was not supposed to be in the Haunted Woods. The plan was to see Edna and be gone before anyone noticed her. But the voice sounded small and afraid.

"Oh, please," it whimpered again. "I need help."

Nomi couldn't stay quiet any longer. "Where are you?" she called out. "Keep talking so I can follow your voice!"

"Oh, thank you!" the little voice piped up. "I'm over here! Come quickly, I'm stuck!"

Trailing the voice through the dense thicket, Nomi finally spotted a small tuft of purple fur poking out through a tangle of branches overhead. She darted over to the tree.

Intertwined in the long arms of the old, gnarled tree was a tiny Poogle. Nomi flew up and perched on a branch next to him. He was a little scratched up, but mostly just terrified, panting frantically with fear. When he caught sight of Nomi, his eyes grew wide with relief.

"A light faerie! What luck," the young Poogle gushed. He struggled to wave, but the branches kept his arms clamped down. "Oh, please hurry and set me free!"

Nomi didn't think she had the strength to move the branches alone. For the millionth time in her life, she wished she was a powerful faerie so she could use her magic to help the little Poogle. But until she returned to Edna, she had no choice. Slowly, one by one, she began to shift the long, heavy branches.

The Poogle looked up at her with big, unblinking eyes.

"Please hurry," he urged. "Balthazar will come back for me soon."

Nomi shivered at the sound of the evil Lupe's name. Knowing that he was nearby sent chills down her wings.

"He is after me," the Poogle continued. "And he'll hurt me. Can't you use your magic to free me?"

"I'm so sorry," Nomi said. "I wish I could, but my faerie powers are not strong." Then she lowered her head. "I'm not supposed to be here," she whispered.

"Well, that makes two of us. My name is Telos," the Poogle told Nomi. "What is your name?"

"Nomi," she said. She dragged a few more branches away from the Poogle. "What happened to you?"

"Balthazar was chasing me. He thought

that I stole something of his. But I didn't. I'm innocent! I was gathering some gnome shrooms with my sisters. They managed to escape, but I got caught here." Telos was chattering so quickly that Nomi had a hard time keeping up.

"Please, just help me get free of these branches," Telos begged. "He saw I was tangled up here and he's coming back for me. You have to hurry."

"I'll try my best to get you out of there," Nomi said. "I just need you to stay calm."

Nomi looked around in despair. She knew that she was never going to be able to move all those branches in time. The only hope of freeing Telos before Balthazar returned was to use magic.

"When I count to three, I want you to try to lift your arms free," she told Telos.

And then, with all her strength, Nomi began to summon her magic. Her power was feeble, but her will to help was great. She hoped with all her heart that she had enough skill to free Telos.

She brought her arms up the way she had seen Mayin do a hundred times. Nomi thought back to her books and remembered the spell to free a captive.

> *"Small helpless Poogle*
>
> *caught in the woods;*
>
> *break free from your tangle;*
>
> *roam as you should."*

As Nomi spoke those words, she felt the last bit of strength draining from her. Her light began to fade and she grew dizzy and too weak to fly. In a flash, she dropped to the ground.

When Nomi fell, Telos jumped up. He was no longer tangled in the branches—and he was no longer a Poogle! Nomi lifted her head just in time to see him grow a long mane, pointy ears, and shifty slanted eyes. Telos had morphed into a Kyrii wearing a black cloak and a large crystal amulet around his neck!

"Well done, Telos," a deep voice called.

Nomi's vision blurred and her head began to spin. As she struggled to remain awake, Nomi spotted a large blue Lupe standing by the tree. It was Balthazar. He stood with a familiar black Crokabek perched on his shoulder, holding a net and a jar.

CHAPTER FIVE

In a flash, Balthazar dropped his net over Nomi. She twisted and turned, but was tangled in the tight weave. Her hands clung to the heavy rope as Balthazar swung the net around to look at her. When she met Balthazar's piercing eyes, she let out a terrified scream.

"That's not going to do you any good," Balthazar told her. "You're on the wrong side of the Faerie City gates now."

Balthazar held the net firmly as he gathered a jar from his pack and placed it on the ground. *This can't be happening!* thought Nomi. *I'm not supposed to be here! This must be a bad dream!*

Without warning, Nomi felt her stomach drop to her feet—like she was zooming down a wet, slick slide. A wash of sickening colors swirled around her as time slowed to a crawl. Nomi glanced at her hand and was shocked to see it growing smaller. She was shrinking!

The next moment Nomi was inside Balthazar's glass jar. Using all her strength, she forced herself to her feet and clawed at the smooth glass around her. A shadow fell on her as Balthazar sealed the mouth of the jar with a heavy oilcloth. *I'm going to suffocate!* she thought, gasping for breath. But then a long, sharp claw punched through the covering, and she was knocked again to the bottom of the jar, greedily drinking in the fresh air that seeped in through the holes.

"Did you put a spell on her already?" Nomi heard Balthazar ask Telos.

"No," Telos answered. "She drained herself trying to free me. Er, me as a Poogle," he corrected himself, shaking his head. "Those light faeries are all pushovers for Poogles. She hardly had any strength left and she used it to help a Poogle she didn't even know."

"Hmm," Balthazar murmured, rolling the jar between his enormous hands. He raised the jar up and peered in at the tiny faerie that lay shaking at the bottom of the jar.

"Maybe she'll be a good match," Telos said, more to himself than Balthazar. He stretched and sighed heavily. "I'm getting too old for all this morphing."

Balthazar wasn't paying attention to the old sorcerer. In his head, he was already thinking about how much this latest light faerie would be worth.

"Now then," Telos said, holding out his hand. "If you would hand me the jar, I need to take care of some important matters." He took off the crystal amulet from his neck.

"First, my payment, Telos. Hand it over and I'll hand over the jar," Balthazar bargained.

Telos raised his thick, bushy eyebrows. "Ah," he said with a twisted smile. "All business, as usual. Such a pity. If you leave now, you'll miss the most interesting part." He passed Balthazar a heavy bag filled with gold coins.

"Whatever you say," Balthazar muttered. He didn't much care what happened next. He had done his job—trapped the faerie, shrunk her down, and handed her over—and was now satisfied to leave. The high price the sorcerer paid for her was the only thing on his mind. Still, Telos was a steady client, and keeping him happy meant a steady stream of gold. Balthazar dropped the heavy bag and leaned against a tree. "Go on, I'm watching," he said with a wave of his hand.

Telos peered into the jar. "I'm terribly sorry to have to do this to you, little light faerie," he said mockingly, "but I am very much hoping your faerie essence will match my mistress's. Then she'll be able to absorb it and perform her own magic once again. She must have all her strength back to carry out the grand plan."

Telos pulled the covering from the top of the jar and jammed his dirty hand inside. Nomi darted about trying to avoid his grasp until she exhausted herself and fell once more to the bottom of the jar.

Roughly, Telos closed his hand around Nomi. From inside his fist, Nomi clawed and scratched at Telos's thick fingers, but he barely seemed to notice. With his other hand, he dropped the crystal amulet into the jar and firmly pressed Nomi against it. Then he spoke a spell she had never heard before:

"Capture the essence of this faerie's light;
leave her as dim as a dark, moonless night."

Instantly, Nomi felt a deep, aching cold filling her body.

"There we go," Telos murmured. "Too bad your wings will wither and your color will fade after I take what I need from you. Not that your faerie essence seemed to be doing you much good anyway. That was the most pathetic little display of magic I've seen in many a moon!" Telos threw back his head and laughed wickedly.

Balthazar watched with increasing interest as the crystal in the amulet began to glow. As it grew brighter, Nomi's wings crumpled and disappeared, and her color slowly drained away. Soon she had turned a dull, grey color and lay slumped and lifeless in the jar.

"That was fast," Balthazar noted.

"My spell is potent," Telos explained. He strung the crystal back on the chain and hooked it around his neck. "I have a good feeling about this one. If my mistress can use her essence, she'll be more powerful than ever!"

"Well, just in case, I'll let you know when the next one stumbles into Edna's Tower," Balthazar offered, tossing a chunk of dried bread to the Crokabek on his shoulder.

Inside the jar, Nomi stirred. Her head was

pounding and she could feel a dull ache in the wing roots on her back. She leaped up and began banging on the smooth glass wall around her. She yelled and jumped up and down inside her confines.

"Feisty little thing!" Telos said, chuckling. "She'll settle down after I give her a memory-erasing spell. We can't have her getting free and telling everyone our plans, now can we?"

"Wait," Nomi shouted. "Please, stop!"

Telos paid no attention as he spoke the final words to erase her memory:

"No knowledge of her past will I leave,
as I am the Master of Memory Thieves."

Telos finished his spell and Nomi lay still once more.

Telos handed the jar back to Balthazar and said, "Leave this in the tree's hollow up there."

"You're not taking her with you now?" Balthazar asked, surprised.

"I have something I must do," the sorcerer said vaguely. "I'll send someone to collect her shortly." Telos nodded a curt farewell and disappeared into the dark woods.

Balthazar stuffed the jar in the hole in the tree. For a moment he paused, sniffing the air. Then, stopping only to grab the heavy bag of coins, he slipped away into the darkness and out of sight.

CHAPTER SIX

Nomi rolled over, banging her head against the hard glass. She rubbed her forehead and moaned.

Where am I?

Slowly, she sat up and pulled her knees to her chest, wrapping her arms tightly around them. Fighting off the tears she felt welling up in her eyes, she stared into the darkness, trying to make out any familiar shape or landmark. Nomi struggled to remember anything about this strange place. Why she was here. Or even where she had come from. All she knew for certain was that she wasn't supposed to be here. A pit of loneliness in her belly told her that home was a long way away. And the ache in her shoulder blades told her that something else was terribly wrong.

Nomi closed her eyes and began to cry. Big tears were rolling down her cheeks when she heard voices nearby. Her head snapped up and she became still once again, bracing herself for whoever was approaching.

"I got you!"

"You so did not!"

Nomi sprang to her feet. Her mind must be playing tricks on her. These voices sounded friendly. *Playful* almost!

"Hey! Check this out!"

Nomi turned to find a huge furry face with

large, soft brown eyes pressed up against the glass of her jar. Trying to get a better view of who was staring at her, she took a few steps back. She wasn't exactly scared, but definitely confused—it was an orange Xweetok staring right at her!

"Look! It's a faerie, Paxi."

Nomi spun around to see another Xweetok racing down from a higher branch. She had matching orange fur and the same friendly brown eyes.

"Wow, Rex, look at her," the Xweetok named Paxi said, examining Nomi through the glass. "I wonder what's wrong with her. She's a really weird color."

Weird color? What does that mean? Nomi wondered. She tried to stand up, but her head began to pound and she collapsed back down.

"Poor little thing," Paxi said, jumping down to the hollow in the tree for a closer look. "I think that she's hurt. Let's try to get her out!"

"Whoa. Look at the holes in the top. It looks like one of Balthazar's jars. I don't know if we should be messing around with this," Rex whispered.

"Don't be such a wimp. Are you going to help or not?" Paxi asked as she wrapped her bushy tail around the jar and began to tug.

"Oh, stop! That will never work!" Rex said. "You jump down to that branch and be ready!"

Paxi spiraled down to a lower branch and looked up just in time to see Rex wrestle the jar out of the hole. He tossed it down to her. Paxi lightly caught the jar and quickly passed it back to Rex, who was already waiting on a branch below. Racing down the tree, the two swiftly and carefully passed the jar between them until they were all safely on the ground.

"Yeehaw!" said Paxi, catching her breath. "Rex, get over here and help me."

Rex held the jar as Paxi tried to unscrew its cover. They gently rolled the jar onto its side, and the tiny faerie tumbled out onto a soft patch of moss.

Almost instantly Nomi began to grow. First her legs stretched out in front of her, then her arms, and soon her body was back to normal size. Paxi and Rex just stared at her as she shook her head, trying to get her bearings. Then, as she slowly got to her feet, she caught sight of her hand and stopped abruptly. Rex and Paxi were right—she was a weird color, or

rather, weirdly *colorless*! Everything about her—her skin, hair, even her fingernails—was grey!

"What's happened to me?" she asked.

Rex stepped forward and tried his best to be calm and reassuring, which for Rex, meant slow and loud.

"WE'RE NOT GOING TO HURT YOU," he shouted. "I'M REX AND THIS IS MY SISTER, PAXI. WHAT'S YOUR NAME?"

Paxi rolled her eyes and flicked Rex with her tail. "She's not deaf, Rex! Just a little . . . out of it."

Nomi stared at the brother and sister Xweetoks. She didn't know how to answer.

Rex circled Nomi. He gave her a sniff. "Hey, are you okay? What's your name?"

"I—I don't know," Nomi said softly. "I can't remember anything." She immediately felt that same tug in her belly reminding her that this was not her home. "I just want to get back to where I'm from."

"Don't worry, we'll help you. Right, Rex?" said Paxi.

"What?" Rex asked, caught off guard. "Oh, of course we will! I've always wanted a bounty hunter on my tail!" Rex turned to look at his fluffy tail. The fur was waving hypnotically in the wind. Looking at it fixedly, Rex sprang up and began chasing it wildly in a circle.

Paxi giggled and gave him a light smack on the head. Instantly, he snapped back into focus. "Sorry," he said, rubbing his head where his sister had bopped him. "We'll help you."

Paxi looked at Nomi. Nomi looked at Rex. And then all three of them began to laugh! Nomi couldn't imagine anything dangerous about these two. *I know I can trust them!* she thought.

Feeling a little more at ease, Nomi looked around at the large leafless trees that surrounded them. Absolutely nothing looked familiar. "What is this place?" she asked.

"This is the Haunted Woods," Rex told her. "Not exactly a resort town for a faerie."

"Rex!" Paxi scolded. Then she turned to Nomi. "I'm sorry about Rex. He doesn't always think before he says things."

"That's all right," said Nomi. Her heart was warming to her new fuzzy friends.

"What's this?" asked Paxi as she picked up the jar and shook it. Something inside rattled.

Nomi reached into the jar. "It's a crystal bracelet," she said, looking at it curiously.

As she turned it over in her hands, Nomi couldn't help admiring its beauty. She showed it to Paxi and asked if she recognized the intricate design etched into it. Paxi examined it for a moment and then handed it to Nomi.

"Look!" she said. "Something is written on it. It says, 'For Nomi. Have the courage to believe in yourself! With love, Mayin.' Do you recognize either of those names?"

Nomi looked down at her feet and slowly shook her head. She was embarrassed she didn't even know her own name.

"It must have fallen off your wrist when you shrank!" Paxi observed. "I think it's a key to your past. For one thing, now you know your name is Nomi."

"You don't look like a Nomi," Rex observed, gnawing on a nut he had just found on the ground.

"Rex!" Paxi scolded again. "Yes, she does. And that's what we'll call her. I think that it's a great name!"

Nomi sat down on a pile of soft leaves.

"Maybe it sounds a little familiar," she said, trying to convince not only her new friends but herself as well. She wrapped a lock of grey hair around her finger in a tight curl.

Paxi nuzzled up beside her. "Don't worry, Nomi. I know your memory will come back soon," she said reassuringly.

"Paxi," said Nomi seriously. "The only thing I know is that I'm lost and I want to go home. I'll do anything to get out of here. But I can't do it without your help."

"Count us in," Paxi said. "Come on, let's get away from this tree. We don't want to be here when that hoodwinker comes back!"

"I'm starving," said Rex, finishing up his nut. "Before we go anywhere, we'd better eat something!" He got up and raced around the tree.

Hearing his words, Nomi realized that she was nearly faint with hunger herself.

"That's a good idea," she agreed. "We have to be ready for whatever journey lies ahead. I have a feeling we'll need to keep up our strength. Rex, where's the nearest place to find food?"

"There are some berry bushes nearby," Rex suggested. "And there's fresh water, too. Do you think that you can walk?"

"I may not remember my name, but I do remember how to walk!" Nomi said gamely. "Let's go!"

CHAPTER SEVEN

Without her wings, Nomi couldn't fly. Instead, she picked her way along the tricky trails and paths, trying to keep up with the agile Xweetoks.

Luckily, her two new friends seemed to be right at home. In fact, they were great traveling companions, chattering all the way and keeping her mind off the hoots and howls of the Haunted Woods.

"We're not supposed to be here either,"

Rex said as they tramped along.

"Really?" asked Nomi. "You seem to know your way around here."

"Well, we live in Neovia, a little village just outside of the Haunted Woods," Paxi explained. "But we come here all the time."

"We like to investigate the spooky spots, to see who gets scared first," Rex added.

Paxi giggled and then continued more seriously, "But if anyone knew we played here, we'd be in big trouble."

Nomi sighed. She looked down and for the first time noticed a small pack on her belt. "Look at this," she said to her new friends.

"Well, what are you waiting for? Open it!" Paxi urged.

"Maybe it will tell you something about who you are!" Rex agreed.

Nomi looked inside the pack and found

a canister full of something black and gritty, and a map labeled HAUNTED WOODS.

"I guess you meant to come here," Paxi said, pointing at the map. "You came prepared." Nomi just shook her head.

"It's all a mystery to me." She picked up the canister of black sand, turning it over in her hands. "I wonder what I was doing with this."

The threesome continued walking on a narrow path and soon the sun began to disappear behind the treetops, a blood-red hue blazing across the sky. Even the sunset in the Haunted Woods was eerie.

As soon as the sun was completely under the horizon, the Woods became clammy and chilly. A large moon slowly rose into the dark sky, creating long, spooky shadows. Nomi shivered in the cold air and hugged her arms close to her chest as she walked.

Rex leaped ahead gathering nuts. Every once in a while he would hand one to Nomi. Paxi continued to be on the lookout with her quick, keen eyes.

"Are the berry bushes far from here?" Nomi asked.

"It shouldn't be too long now," Paxi said. "We turn left up here."

"That's not right," Rex chided. He pointed to a tree farther away. "That's the turn. I know my way around here."

Suddenly a raspy voice interrupted their argument.

"Actually, you're both wrong, it's that way."

"Ahh!" yelled a startled Rex, leaping back and stumbling over a root.

"Says who?" asked Paxi bravely.

"Says me," the voice answered from over their heads. The three friends looked up and spied a small Korbat hanging upside down from a low branch crossing the path.

Paxi and Rex looked at each other and burst out laughing. They fell to the ground and rolled around, their relief making them giddy.

Finally Paxi pulled herself together. "Nomi, Ullia. Ullia, Nomi," she said, wiping her eyes. "Honestly, Ullia, you scared the fur right off of us! We just never know where you'll be hanging around!"

At this, Ullia burst into a contagious giggle.

"Ullia has always lived in the Woods. We met her years ago and she tries to help us stay out of trouble," Rex said with a wink.

"Looks like I'm not doing a very good job—I could hear you two arguing a mile away!" Ullia said, giggling.

Just then, a thought seemed to strike Paxi, and she pulled Nomi aside. "Ullia's a great friend," she whispered. "She has helped us out more times than I can count, and she has got a heck of a sense of direction. It might be good to have her with us."

Nomi nodded. In her position, she wasn't about to turn away anyone who could help. So Nomi and her new friends told Ullia about the day's events. Nomi started by telling her about waking up shrunken and trapped in a jar. Rex chimed in that the jar belonged to Balthazar and described how they had tossed it down the tree. Paxi finished by explaining that Nomi had lost her memory. "And now we're trying to help her get back home!" she concluded breathlessly.

Ullia listened intently, gently fanning her wings. She seemed to be deep in thought.

"I've heard about this before, but didn't pay much attention until now," she said at last.

"What do you mean?" the three asked in unison.

"The rumor is that someone is hunting faeries. And I don't just mean that brute Balthazar. He's just in it for the money. Someone else is stealing the pure essence of the light faerie. They're trying to use it for themselves," Ullia explained. "I'm surprised the thief didn't take you with him. They say there's a place where all of the grey faeries are being held. Nomi, someone may be after you."

A chill shot down Nomi's spine as Ullia's words rang in her ears. Instinctively, she knew they were true.

"I guess that makes sense," Paxi said.

"What do we do now?" Nomi asked.

"I don't know," said Ullia, perking up her ears to listen to the howling sounds coming from deep within the Woods.

"Well, no matter what we do, we still need to eat something," Rex said helpfully.

"All right, you lead the way, Paxi," said Nomi.

"I'll lead the way," said Rex.

"No, *I'll* lead the way," Ullia told them.

As Nomi followed her guides, she tried to remember any little detail of her past that might explain what had happened to her. She couldn't stop thinking about what Ullia had said. Somewhere in the dark Woods, someone was looking for her.

CHAPTER EIGHT

"E veryone still with me?" Ullia asked. She lifted one of her red wings and pointed straight ahead. "Almost there."

Within a few minutes, they came to a small clearing surrounded by bushes. Nomi, Paxi, and Rex raced toward it and began gathering handfuls of berries and nuts. When they had plenty of food, they sat on a log and ate their fill. Rex pointed out a small pool of fresh water with tiny ripples moving along the surface.

Nomi felt content for the first time since she had woken up inside the jar.

Just then a warning squeak came from Ullia, who had been circling above, keeping watch. Nomi turned anxiously to look at Paxi and Rex. They stood as still as statues, except for the quiver of their noses sniffing the air.

"What's going on?" she asked.

"Smells like a Skeith. Ullia?" asked Paxi in a hushed, wobbly voice.

"Quick! Hide! I'll distract him as long as I can," Ullia replied.

As fast as lightning, Paxi and Rex dived under a pile of heavy branches at the edge of the clearing. Nomi froze, not knowing which way to run.

"Nomi, follow us!" Paxi urged.

Nomi sprinted toward the little shelter and dived underneath the branches.

"That was close!" Rex hissed.

Outside, Ullia's squeals were getting dangerously close. The three lay flat on the ground, peering out into the shadows of the night.

Nomi caught sight of Ullia just as she was flying at top speed toward the clouds. Then she stopped, tucked her wings closely into her body, and nose-dived to the ground at a staggering speed. Nomi gasped.

"Just watch," Paxi told her.

Again, the three watched Ullia's outrageous skydiving act.

"What's she doing?" Nomi dared to ask.

Soon enough the question was answered. The ground began to tremble. Nomi's eyes grew wide.

"Are those . . . footsteps?" she whispered to Paxi.

"Shh," Rex cautioned. "He's getting closer!"

The thudding sound grew louder and closer and then, directly in front of their hiding place, four legs stopped—scaly and as big as tree trunks. Nomi grabbed Paxi's and Rex's paws and didn't dare breathe. She could hear the Skeith's huge nostrils huffing and puffing as it sniffed for prey.

Just then, Ullia dive-bombed once more, attacking the Skeith's scaly legs. To her amazement, Nomi saw that there were punctures and scratches in the beast's rough skin. She caught her breath, worried for her brave little friend. But Ullia was much too fast for the giant Skeith.

Over and over, Ullia dived and circled, harrying the Skeith and luring it away from her friends' hiding place. The Skeith swung its mighty head, trying to knock her from the sky, but it was no match for her speed. The faster she flew, the more disoriented the monster seemed to become, as it staggered around the clearing and made the ground shake with its thunderous steps.

Finally, bleeding and dazed, the hunter seemed to give up. As Ullia circled above, shrieking in victory, it turned around and lumbered out of the clearing and back into the Haunted Woods.

"You were incredible, Ullia!" Nomi gushed.

Ullia looked pleased, but then her expression grew sober. "I think he knew you were here, Nomi," she said gravely. "You must have been tracked."

The friends sat in a circle and thought about their next move.

"Whoever sent that guy meant business,"

said Paxi. "Ullia, what's your call?"

"We need to get Nomi back to her home—fast! I don't know how to do it, but I know who will. We must consult the Brain Tree!" Ullia exclaimed.

"What's that?" Nomi asked, surprised.

"He's the smartest tree ever!" Rex chimed in. "We've never seen him, but he knows everything!"

"He's the oldest tree in the Haunted Woods—hundreds of years old! During all those years, he has absorbed a great deal of knowledge," Ullia continued.

"That's perfect," Nomi exclaimed. "Do you think the tree can tell me what happened to me . . . and how to get home?"

"Well, hopefully," Ullia said gently.

"What do you mean?" Nomi asked.

"The tree's knowledge isn't free. Before he will tell you what you want to know, you'll need to prove yourself by answering a question. And those questions are never easy!"

Nomi felt her mouth go dry. How could she hope to answer the tree's questions if she didn't even know who she was? But there was no other choice.

"Let's go find the Brain Tree," she said bravely. "I want to go home!"

CHAPTER NINE

With a plan in place, the four set out once again through the ragged underbrush of the Woods. Rex raced ahead, zipping around the trees and bushes. Ullia flew overhead. Nomi and Paxi traveled side by side.

As they walked along, Paxi noticed Nomi's furrowed brow.

"Are you worried about the Brain Tree?" she asked.

Nomi nodded. "What if I don't know the answer to his question? What if I can't get home?" Nomi blurted out.

Paxi gave Nomi an encouraging wink.

"It's going to be fine, Nomi, you'll see," she said. "That bracelet of yours seems to have some pretty good advice for you."

Nomi turned and looked at her curiously. She had forgotten all about the bracelet! *Have the courage to believe in yourself* . . . She took it off and lightly ran her fingers over the inscription. *Maybe this really is the key to my past—and my future, too!*

After many hours of walking, Nomi noticed that the scenery around them began to change. The roots underfoot were growing sparse and spindly, and the trees seemed weak and oddly vulnerable.

"Why is it different here?" Nomi asked.

"As we get closer to the Brain Tree, his life force begins to take over," Ullia explained. "He needs a lot of nourishment to keep his brain going. Nothing else can grow strong here."

Nomi had been watching her feet to avoid stumbling over the twisted roots and stones underfoot, but when she looked up, she saw the most astonishing sight of her life.

"The Brain Tree!" Ullia announced.

Nomi couldn't take her eyes off it. The trunk was thick and solid. Dark brown slabs of bark provided a heavy armor. The trunk was astonishing, but hardly the most impressive part of this grand tree. Out of it bulged an enormous brain, and below that Nomi could make out a pair of closed eyes and a long, wrinkly mouth.

Suddenly, the tree's eyes flew open and it stared fiercely in Nomi's direction.

"Who goes there?" the Brain Tree asked.

The tree's voice was so powerful that it blew Nomi's long hair back and she struggled to stay on her feet. Mustering all her strength, Nomi spoke.

"Brain Tree, I've come here seeking knowledge," she said, repeating the words Ullia had helped her memorize.

The Tree's eyes glowed.

"What kind of knowledge?" the Tree asked.

"Someone in the Haunted Woods has stolen my powers and erased my memory. I need to know where I am from, Mr. Tree," Nomi explained. "Please tell me how to get home."

The Brain Tree's eyes dimmed and he was silent for several moments as he pondered Nomi's question. Finally, he opened his red eyes once again. "Before I tell you, I need you

to answer a question. My knowledge comes at a price!" the Brain Tree boomed.

"I'm ready," Nomi replied.

"This is your question: What was given to you, belongs to only you, but is used by your friends more than yourself?"

Nomi panicked. *What kind of question is that?*

Desperately searching for clues, Nomi looked around at her friends. Paxi and Rex looked back at her with unquestioning eyes, urging her on. Ullia was flying nearby, on constant duty as their trustworthy guard.

Her heart sinking, Nomi thought back on the quest on which she had embarked with her new friends. They had shared laughter, encouraged each other, struggled together, and even provided safety for one another.

They've helped me so much.

Nomi closed her eyes, trying to summon the strength to tell her friends that she could not answer the question. *How can I let them down now?* she wondered sadly.

She thought back to the moment Paxi and Rex had freed her from Balthazar's jar. She remembered again how Paxi had found the crystal bracelet, and how she had shown her the words engraved inside. Suddenly, Nomi's eyes flew open and her face lit up.

That's it! Giggling joyfully, Nomi knew she had the right answer!

"Well, that's easy!" Nomi told the Brain Tree. "I may not remember where I'm from, but with the help of my friends, I know who I am."

"What is your answer?" the Brain Tree asked.

"My name!" Nomi said triumphantly. "It was given to me, belongs to me, but is used by my friends!"

Paxi, Rex, and Ullia turned and looked with wide eyes at the giant Tree.

"You have answered correctly, Nomi," the Brain Tree replied. "And for this, I will tell you how to get to Faerieland—your home."

Ullia, Paxi, and Rex jumped up and down with delight.

"Your way lies to the southeast," the Tree continued. "Follow this path, and you will find your way out of the Haunted Woods. Then you must continue on until you reach the coast. From there, as you look into the clouds, you shall see the land from whence you came. Best of luck." With that, the Tree's eyes closed and he was silent.

"Thank you, Mr. Tree," Nomi said. She and her friends ran toward the path the Tree had indicated, their hearts bursting with relief and anticipation. But suddenly Nomi stopped and ran back.

"Wait!" she called out. "I don't have any wings. How will we get to Faerieland?"

But the Brain Tree did not respond. Deep, resonant snores began to issue from his wrinkled mouth.

Paxi walked over to Nomi. "Don't worry," she said reassuringly. "We've gotten this far. I'm sure we'll figure it out when the time comes."

Feeling lighter than she had since she had arrived in the Haunted Woods, Nomi led her friends down the path. She had a strong feeling that someone was waiting for her at home. And that someone would know how to help her get her magic back.

The four travelers quickened their pace with a new sense of hope. The sun was beginning to rise, and they had to find a place to rest. They would need all their strength for the long journey that awaited them.